Granny Grimm's Gruesome Glasses

Jenny Nimmo and David Wynn Millward

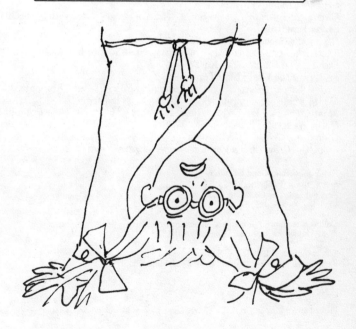

Collins

Best Friends · *Jessy and the Bridesmaid's Dress* ·
Jessy Runs Away · **Rachel Anderson**
Changing Charlie · *Clogpots in Space* · **Scoular Anderson**
Ernest the Heroic Lion-tamer · **Damon Burnard**
Weedy Me · **Sally Christie**
Something Old · **Ruth Craft**
Almost Goodbye Guzzler · *Two Hoots* · **Helen Cresswell**
Magic Mash · *Nina's Machines* · **Peter Firmin**
Shadows on the Barn · **Sarah Garland**
Clever Trevor · *Nora Bone* · *Nora Bone and the Tooth Fairy* · **Brough Girling**
Private Eye of New York · *Sharon and Darren* · **Nigel Gray**
The Thing-in-a-Box · **Diana Hendry**
Desperate for a Dog · *Houdini Dog* · *More Dog Trouble* · **Rose Impey**
Georgie and the Computer Bugs · *Georgie and the Dragon* ·
Georgie and the Planet Raider · **Julia Jarman**
Cowardy Cowardy Cutlass · *Cutlass Rules the Waves* · *Free With Every Pack* ·
Mo and the Mummy Case · *The Fizziness Business* · **Robin Kingsland**
Albertine, Goose Queen · *And Pigs Might Fly!* · *Jigger's Day Off* ·
Martians at Mudpuddle Farm · *Mossop's Last Chance* · **Michael Morpurgo**
Granny Grimm's Gruesome Glasses · **Jenny Nimmo**
Grubble Trouble · **Hilda Offen**
Hiccup Harry · *Harry Moves House* · *Harry's Party* · *Harry with Spots On* ·
Chris Powling
Grandad's Concrete Garden · **Shoo Rayner**
The Father Christmas Trap · **Margaret Stonborough**
Our Toilet's Haunted · **John Talbot**
Pesters of the West · **Lisa Taylor**
Jacko · *Lost Property* . *Messages* · *Rhyming Russell* · **Pat Thomson**
Monty Ahoy! · *Monty Bites Back* · *Monty must be Magic !* ·
Monty, The Dog Who Wears Glasses · *Monty – Up To His Neck in Trouble* ·
Colin West
Ging Gang Goolie - It's An Alien ·
Stone the Crows, It's a Vacuum-cleaner · **Bob Wilson**

First published in Great Britain by
A & C Black (Publishers) Ltd 1995
First published by Collins in 1995
10 9 8 7 6 5 4 3 2 1

Collins is an imprint of HarperCollins*Publishers* Ltd
77-85 Fulham Palace Road, London W6 8JB.

Text copyright © 1995 Jenny Nimmo
Illustrations copyright © 1995 David Wynn Millward
All rights reserved.

ISBN 0-00-675107-5

Printed and bound in Great Britain by HarperCollins Manufacturing, Glasgow

Chapter 1

Fiona Smiley lived in a ramshackle house with broken gutters and dirty windows.

The paint was peeling and the gate wouldn't close properly.

No one in Fiona's family had time to mend things. They were always too busy being brainy.

4

Her father was a Professor of
Ancient History.

Her mother spoke nine languages
and often advised the government
on foreign affairs.

Her brother, Brian, was a computer wizard. Fiona thought he was even beginning to look like a computer.

Fiona hated not being brainy. She
wondered if braininess had
something to do with wearing
glasses. Her mother, her father and
her brother all wore glasses but
none of them would let her borrow
theirs.

So, one night,
when they were
asleep, Fiona
tiptoed around the
house trying on
all their glasses.

But it was no use.
Brian's made things look too big.

Professor Smiley's glasses turned
things upside-down . . .

. . . and Mrs Smiley's carried things
so far away, Fiona couldn't see
them at all.

So next morning, Fiona went to the chemist's on her way to school to buy herself a pair of glasses.

She chose a pair of glasses with huge blue frames and rose-tinted lenses. Fiona thought they made her look really brainy.

But her friend, Tracy, said she looked 'naff'.

Arguing always gave Fiona a headache, and the glasses didn't help one bit when she tried to do her fractions.

Fiona stomped home feeling really miserable. But just as she was trying to close her garden gate, something caught her eye – A PAIR OF GLASSES!

They were sitting on the wall right in front of her,

a pair of neat gold-rimmed glasses just her size!

Fiona was too excited to notice Granny Grimm, who owned the glasses, standing on the other side of the wall.

Hold the bus, Sophie. I've got something in my eye.

BUS STOP

Gold-rimmed glasses! Maybe they'll do the trick..

Without stopping to think, Fiona
snatched off her rose-tinted glasses
and put on the gold-rimmed pair.

When Fiona put on the glasses,
things didn't just look different.
They FELT different.

Fiona tried to run towards her house, but her legs felt peculiar. And when she looked down to see what had happened, she found that the only Fiona-ish things about her were her feet.

Just then, Brian came outside, and believing Granny Grimm to be Fiona, called her in for tea.

Granny Grimm, who never refused an invitation, ran after Brian, into Fiona's house and into Fiona's life. While Fiona stood by, too dizzy to move.

Chapter 2

Fiona tried to shout at Brian, but her voice made a croaky sound and no words came out. She was about to chase after him when a girl grabbed hold of her arm and dragged her towards a bus.

The girl took no notice of Fiona's feeble cries and Fiona was too weak to escape. Before she knew what was happening, the girl had shoved her on to the bus.

Fiona stood in the aisle feeling
horribly breathless.

Have my seat, Granny Grimm.
Give your legs a rest.

I don't want
your seat, I'm
a child.

Come on, Gran.
Don't be difficult

Fiona tried
to keep calm.
She had
been turned
into someone
else. Transbodified. Perhaps it had
something to do with the glasses?
She gave the glasses a tug. They
wouldn't budge. They seemed to be
glued to her skin. Fiona gave a
loud moan.

THEY'RE STUCK!

At the next stop the girl, who seemed to be Fiona's minder, pulled Fiona to her feet and guided her firmly off the bus.

Fiona didn't have the strength to run away. She followed the girl into a strange house and sat down at a long table in a very tidy kitchen. Besides the girl, whose name was Sophie, there were three other people in the kitchen. A boy of about eight, an almost middle-aged man, and a small blonde woman.

All the Grimms were very neat and tidy and didn't smile much. None of them wore glasses. When Fiona tried to tell them that she was not Granny Grimm, they didn't believe her.

Mrs Grimm just put a plate of horrible-looking food in front of her.

Chapter 3

After tea Fiona was helped into the sitting room and plonked in front of the television.

Fiona didn't like to argue with Mrs Grimm, so she took the cardigan and began to knit.

It took Fiona less than an hour to finish the cardigan. She seemed to have inherited Granny Grimm's gift for speed-knitting.

Mrs Grimm and Sophie helped Fiona upstairs to her room.

Suddenly Sophie noticed Fiona's trainers.

Mrs Grimm and Sophie left the room looking very cross, and Fiona was left alone.

She tugged at the glasses.

When Fiona saw the intercom she had a brilliant idea. She waited until the whole house was asleep, and then shouted the rudest words she could think of. Words that most grannies probably hadn't even heard of.

Exhausted by her dreadful evening
Fiona lay back and drifted off to
sleep, wondering if
the real Granny
Grimm was enjoying
being Fiona.

Chapter 4

When Fiona woke up she thought that she was back in her own room with the peeling wallpaper and the friendly mouse. But it was only an illusion. She could hear Sophie and Sam getting ready for school and longed to be with them.

She got out of bed as fast as she could, and put on her clothes.

When she was dressed, Fiona crept downstairs without making a sound.

Fiona wrenched open the door and made a dash for the gate. She tried leapfrogging, a talent for which she'd been famous, but her legs weren't as supple as they used to be.

Fiona trudged up to her room without stopping to have her breakfast. She had never realized how stiff old people's legs could become.

At eleven o'clock Mrs Grimm brought her a cup of tea and a biscuit.

For lunch Fiona was given hard peas and something that looked like boot leather.

After their meal Mrs Grimm took Fiona shopping. This involved a great deal of queuing, and Fiona wished she could have brought a walking stick.

Just as they were leaving Savepounds Supermarket, Fiona saw an amazing sight. There, bold as brass, was Brian, HOLDING HANDS WITH A GIRL! Fiona leapt towards him. After a struggle, Brian managed to tear himself away and Fiona was led home in disgrace.

That evening she lay in her gloomy room, listening to the Grimms grumbling voices in the room below.

Sam brought Fiona a cup of cocoa before he went to bed. He didn't seem as grim as the rest of the family so Fiona decided to ask for his help.

Fiona drew a picture of herself as she used to be, so that Sam would recognize her.

Chapter 5

The next day, Fiona didn't attempt to leave the house. She waited eagerly for Sam's report. Mrs Grimm made her watch television, but when she had gone, Fiona switched it off.

How to mend dripping Taps → What you need:
① TAP WASHER
② ADJUSTABLE SPANNERS

A) OPEN TAP
B) REMOVE TAP TOP
C) TAKE OUT PLUNGER
D) REPLACE WASHER
E) RE-ASSEMBLE

NUT

NEW WASHER

OLD FLAT OR SPLIT WASHER (DISCARD)

← DRIP DRY

How to screw down loose window-catches
What you need ① SCREW-DRIVER ② SCREW

CATCH
WINDOW

Ⓐ PLACE NEW SCREW IN SCREW-HOLE.
Ⓑ SCREW IT UP.

She looked for something else to do. In a corner of the room she found a pile of D.I.Y. magazines. Fiona settled down to read. It was fascinating. She discovered all the things she'd longed to know.

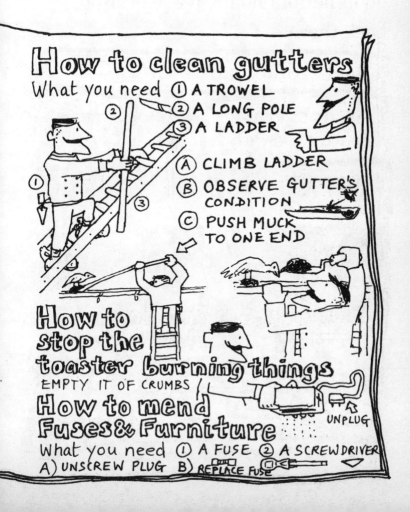

Fiona was so absorbed in the magazines she didn't hear Sophie and Sam come home from school. And when they had tea, she didn't hear a word anyone said. She was thinking of all the things she could do in her old home, if she ever got back there.

After tea, Sam came up to Fiona's room. 'I've seen a girl just like the one in your picture,' he told Fiona. 'She was in the park.'

'I ran up to her and told her she was my gran,' Sam said, 'but she didn't agree. And her friend told me to leave her alone or she'd go to the police.'

The next day Mrs Grimm took
Fiona to the post office to fetch her
pension.

While Mrs Grimm was queuing for
fish, Fiona slipped into the D.I.Y.
shop next door.

The man behind the counter looked
rather surprised when he saw
Fiona's list.

One large hammer

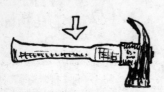

Three dozen
medium-sized nails

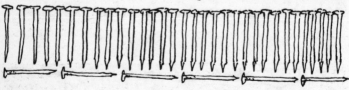

Tube of wood glue
3 spanners
in different sizes

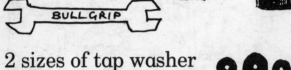

BULLGRIP

STICK WOOD GLUE

2 sizes of tap washer
Fuses

40

Mrs Grimm was very suspicious of Fiona's bulging D.I.Y. bag.

When she got home, Fiona rushed
upstairs and hid the bag under the
bed.

Chapter 6

On Saturday morning, Sam kept his word and took Fiona to Savepounds Supermarket. And there, standing by the entrance, was Fiona, or rather Granny Grimm looking like Fiona.

Granny Grimm was now very
nimble, even in her granny shoes.
She nipped into the supermarket
and vanished into a sea of trolleys.

Sam and Fiona chased after Granny Grimm. But they couldn't catch the now agile granny.

Fiona began to feel breathless, her old bones were playing up.

Granny Grimm slipped out of
Fiona's grasp, leaving her holding
nothing but a red ribbon.

Fiona was so exhausted after the long chase, Sam agreed to wheel her home in the trolley.

Fiona had never felt so disheartened in her whole life. But there was worse to come.

When they got home, Mrs Grimm
was looking grimmer than ever.

Fiona almost fainted when she saw the list of things she had to pack.

LIST

2 prs long pants

2 prs thick vests

2 cardis

Woollen hat

2 prs wool tights

1 nice dress

2 thick nighties

Duffle coat

2 petticoats

1 thick scarf

Walking boots

Hot water bottle COSY

AND DON'T FORGET YOUR KNITTING!

Fiona spent the weekend in a daze.
With a heavy heart she washed and
ironed the clothes she'd been told
to pack.

On Sunday afternoon, Fiona felt so gloomy she flopped down in a big armchair and turned on the television. The doorbell rang but she took no notice. And then Sam appeared.

It's for you.

Who is it?

It's a surprise.

I hope it's a nice one.

Sam winked at Fiona as she passed him. Fiona was mystified – who would want to visit her? As she reached the open front door, she couldn't believe her eyes, for there, on the step was the real Granny Grimm.

Sam suggested that Fiona and Granny Grimm swop glasses at exactly the same moment.

Off came Granny Grimm's gruesome glasses.
Off came the rose-tinted glasses.

Just for a moment Sam was
confused. Then he saw the shoes
and he knew who was who.

He ran to get Fiona's D.I.Y. bag and
when Granny Grimm heard where
her pension money had gone, she
gave Fiona her wholehearted
approval.

You need it, dear.

Before she left, Fiona asked Sam to make a promise.

And then Granny Grimm took Fiona back to her ramshackle house.

When Fiona entered the house, she was surprised to find Brian cowering behind a chair in the sitting room.

When Fiona had dealt with Brian
she started fixing the house.

First she changed
the tap washer.

Then she mended
the fuse.

She cleaned
the gutter.

She fixed the
broken chair.

She patched
the cracks
in the wall.

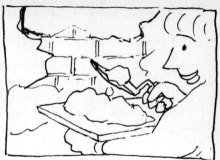

And then
she set to
work in the
garden.

Of course, Professor and Mrs
Smiley were far too busy to notice
Fiona doing all these things.
But Brian was most impressed.

In no time at all the ramshackle house was really comfortable. Fiona became quite famous for doing-it-herself. She could mend anything, anywhere, and before long she had earned enough money to buy herself a workbench, a power drill and a tool-box with spanners and screwdrivers in seven different sizes.

Be a darling and fix my door.

Fi, I can't work my stereo!

Fi, darling, can you mend my typewriter?

63

A month later, Fiona invited Sam and Granny Grimm to tea, and they all agreed that life was pretty good.